LEGENDS OF CHIMA™

GORILLAS GONE BANANAS

Scholastic Inc.

"A Groovy Day," "Basic Training," and "The Auction" written by Greg Farshtey. Adapted by Anna Holmes.

Illustrated by Ameet Studio

ISBN 978-0-545-51752-2

LEGO, the LEGO logo, the Brick and Knob configurations, the Minifigure and LEGENDS OF CHIMA are trademarks of the LEGO Group. ©2013 The LEGO Group. Produced by Scholastic Inc. under license from the LEGO Group.

Published by Scholastic Inc. SCHOLASTIC and associated logos are trademarks and/or registered trademarks of Scholastic Inc.

12 11 10 9 8 7 6 5 4 3 2 1   13 14 15 16 17 18/0

Printed in the U.S.A.   40
First Scholastic printing, September 2013

MIX
Paper from responsible sources
FSC™ C020056

TABLE OF CONTENTS

FIGHTING FOR CHIMA

Welcome to the land of Chima. For hundreds of years, this kingdom was a peaceful place. But that was before the great conflict. Now a fierce battle rages on, turning friends into enemies and pitting tribe against tribe. We have rebuilt our vehicles to use them as fighting machines. The woods, plains, and jungles are places of peril. Chima has become a battlefield.

One thing, though, has not changed. The CHI—Chima's most precious energy source. We Lions continue to collect CHI Orbs in the Sacred Pool. Once a month, we share the CHI evenly among all the tribes despite the battles we fight. CHI must be used equally; otherwise untold calamities will befall Chima.

I am LaGravis, the king of the Lions. My tribe guards the CHI against the devious attacks of the Crocodiles, Wolves, and Ravens. We will defend our world and its ancient traditions no matter what it takes. But we could not do it without the powerful help of our allies.

THE GORILLAS

The Gorillas are possibly the strongest and most agile warriors in Chima. If they wanted, they could easily defeat just about any other tribe in the land. However, they are not warriors by nature. They prefer to live in harmony with the world and spend hours each day meditating in a state they call "the Great Mellow."

The peaceful members of this tribe live in the jungle treetops, swinging from branch to branch and admiring all of nature's wonders. A Gorilla could pass an entire afternoon watching a flower grow.

But when the safety of Chima is threatened, Gorillas will do everything they can to protect the land they love. Using their incredible strength and lightning-fast reflexes, Gorillas can defeat even the most experienced warriors. And their battle machines are modeled after their own bodies, capable of pummeling an entire army in seconds. We Lions are very lucky to have the Gorillas at our side.

Despite his intimidating appearance, Gorzan the Gorilla is actually one of the most soft-hearted creatures in Chima. He is incredibly powerful and can defeat an enemy in seconds, but he will later anguish over "the poor plants" he stepped on during the battle.

Gorzan is extremely sensitive and spends most of his time watching flowers. He sometimes feels another creature's pain before they even realize they *had* any pain. And his favorite way to greet everyone is with a big bear hug. Gorzan is close friends with my son, Laval. He was once friends with Cragger the Crocodile Prince, too. That is, until Cragger turned vicious in his quest to control all the CHI. Gorzan's warrior instincts kick in the moment someone threatens one of his friends . . . or tramples his favorite flowers.

LaGravis says:

Though Gorzan fights to protect Chima from the Crocs, Wolves, and Ravens, he still believes there is good in every animal, including his enemies.

THE RAVENS

The Ravens are a very sneaky tribe. They are also one of the greediest in Chima. These sharp-tongued thieves can't keep themselves from stealing, regardless of the value of the things they suddenly decide to "take care of." Being on friendly terms with the Ravens doesn't help—they steal as much from their friends as from their enemies.

They will be more than happy to sell someone back their missing item at a "fair price." If you're lucky, you may even get a discount! That's how the Ravens make a deal. No amount of arguing will get a Raven to admit he's stolen your property—in fact, he'll insist he's giving you a break by offering it for half price!

But don't underestimate these crafty birds' fighting abilities. They can be vicious opponents, especially if there's a profit to be turned. Greed for reward is the only reason the Raven Tribe has allied with the Crocodiles in their fight for the CHI.

RAZAR

Razar the Raven has swindled every single member of his tribe at least once—and they all respect him greatly for it. After all, Razar is a keen follower of his family's traditions: His parents sold him more than seventeen times (and then stole him back, so they could sell him again).

Razar has a metal hook in place of one hand. No one knows how he lost it . . . perhaps he just traded it. Razar loves wheeling, dealing, and stealing. And no matter what, he'll insist he's "cutting you a deal!"

Razar never does anything that doesn't somehow benefit him. That's why he had the Raven Tribe join with Cragger in the battle for CHI. He's certain he can turn a profit when the dust settles. Razar is a pure mercenary who will fight for the highest bidder . . . and then steal all their weapons while they're not looking.

LaGravis says:

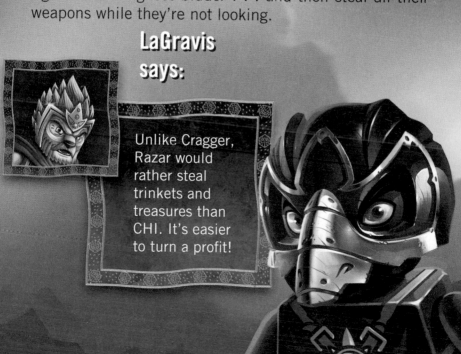

Unlike Cragger, Razar would rather steal trinkets and treasures than CHI. It's easier to turn a profit!

TURN THE PAGE
FOR **THREE**
EXCITING
LEGENDS OF
™
CHIMA
STORIES!

A GROOVY DAY

It was a warm, sunny morning in Chima. Gorzan the Gorilla smiled as he headed up a steep rocky path along one of Chima's tallest mountains. Little did he know, danger lurked directly behind him.

This is too easy, thought Wilhurt the Wolf as he followed Gorzan. *That foolish Gorilla is going to lead me right to his hidden stash of CHI!*

Earlier that morning, Wilhurt had heard a rumor among the Wolf Pack that the Gorillas were hiding a large stockpile of CHI in a new secret location. Then, Wilhurt spotted Gorzan walking through the forest. He realized this was his chance. Surely the Gorilla was heading straight to check on the new hiding place of the CHI!

All I have to do is follow him, and their CHI is ours, Wilhurt thought with a wicked grin.

Quietly, the Wolf trailed Gorzan. He made sure to keep his distance but always had the Gorilla in sight. Wilhurt climbed farther and farther up the mountain, following Gorzan until they reached a narrow ledge. Suddenly, a giant boulder fell directly behind them!

The ground shook as the rock smashed onto the trail. The path back down the mountain was completely blocked.

"Whoa!" exclaimed Wilhurt, jumping clear. Then he gasped. He'd just given himself away.

To Wilhurt's surprise, Gorzan slowly turned and smiled brightly at him.

"Oh, hey there, Wolf-*dude*," Gorzan said. "Didn't see you there. Great view, huh?"

"Great . . . what?" Wilhurt stammered.

"From up here, you can see *all* of Chima." Gorzan held his arms out wide. "Times like this, you really feel one with the Great Mellow, you know?"

"The great . . . *what*?" sputtered Wilhurt. Then he growled. "Enough messing around, Gorilla. Show me where your hidden CHI stash is!"

Gorzan shook his head, still smiling. "Aw, come on; take a little time to relax. Enjoy the fresh air. Be one with the Great Mellow. You know, we Gorillas have a saying . . ."

Gorzan then proceeded to explain at length the Gorilla Tribe's philosophy about nature, harmony, and the meaning of life in general.

The next three hours did not go well for Wilhurt. No matter how hard he tried, he couldn't get Gorzan to reveal the secret location of the CHI. The Gorilla just kept going on and on about how all the animals in Chima were "brothers and sisters" to one another, under their fur . . . or feathers . . . or scales. The more Wilhurt snarled and snapped, the more Gorzan talked about peace, love, and understanding.

As the sun sank lower in the sky, Wilhurt couldn't take it anymore. He was trapped on a ledge with a Gorilla who wouldn't stop talking, and it was driving him crazy.

I don't care about the CHI at this point, he thought desperately. *I just need to get past that boulder and* down the mountain. *Or make that Gorilla stop talking.* Wilhurt glanced over the side of the ledge. The soft, leafy treetops weren't that far below them. *What if I give him a little push?* Wilhurt thought. *He'll land on the trees below. He'll be fine. Gorillas do it all the time. And then I'll finally have some silence!*

"Hey, look, down there," Wilhurt said. "I see, um, a Lion and a Crocodile hugging!"

Gorzan beamed. "Where? Where?" he asked, leaning forward.

Quickly, Wilhurt ran at Gorzan and pushed with all his might. But the Gorilla was so big and strong that he never even felt Wilhurt's shoves.

"Can't see it, but it must have been a sight." Gorzan sighed. "Hey, maybe we should hug, too, Wilhurt!"

"Uh . . . sure thing," Wilhurt replied, already hatching a plan. When Gorzan turned to him, arms outstretched, Wilhurt threw himself at the Gorilla, intending to knock him off the ledge. Instead, Wilhurt just bounced right off.

Gorzan laughed. "Is that how you hug in the Wolf Pack? I've never seen that before, but there's room in the Great Mellow for all kinds of new things. Why, just the other day, I was saying, 'I bet the Wolves aren't as bad as everyone thinks. They just need somebody to hold out a paw.' Right?"

"Yeah, right," growled Wilhurt. He was starting to get a headache. He didn't know how much longer he could take of this. "You know, we might get a better view from up higher," Wilhurt suggested. "Why don't you climb up, and then you can reach down and pull me after you. Right, um . . . er . . . brother?"

Gorzan's face lit up. "That's a great idea!" he exclaimed.

Wilhurt chuckled. He thought it was a great idea, too. Since the rock face above them was almost sheer, Gorzan was sure to slip and fall if he tried to climb it.

Gorzan made a good effort, but there were hardly any handholds. Twice, he almost lost his grip and tumbled off the mountain. But both times he caught himself before he fell.

"Maybe I can . . . give you a boost?" Wilhurt suggested. He grabbed one of Gorzan's legs and tugged with all his might, hoping to pull the Gorilla off the mountain. To his surprise, Gorzan started laughing. Then Gorzan kicked out his leg, slamming Wilhurt into the rocks alongside the path.

"Sorry, brother," Gorzan apologized. "I'm ticklish there."

By now, Wilhurt was really desperate. He peered back over the ledge. *The trees aren't that far away*, he thought. *I think I can make it if I jump. All I know is I can't stay up here with this Gorilla one more second!*

Taking a deep breath, Wilhurt jumped.

"Owww! Ouch! *Owoo!*" Wilhurt howled loudly as he bounced off the mountain and crashed through the tree leaves. He hit the ground with an "Oof!" and lay still. He had made it. He was off the mountain. And away from the Gorilla.

Wilhurt was just breathing a sigh of relief when, suddenly, there was Gorzan swinging easily down through the trees to land beside him.

"Hey, Wolf-dude!" Gorzan called. "Cool jump. You just trusted yourself to nature, huh? That's the best way to be one with the Great Mellow."

"Wait a minute!" shouted Wilhurt. "How did you get down here so fast? We were trapped up there!"

"Trapped?" Gorzan asked, scratching his head. "I wasn't trapped. I go up there all the time. I just took the shortcut to get down."

Wilhurt thought his head would explode. "Then why didn't you say we could get down? We've been up there the entire day!"

"I know." Gorzan smiled. "It was awesome, wasn't it? We should do this all the time. You know, the Great Mellow has a saying . . ."

Wilhurt got to his feet and ran through the jungle as fast as he could. He zipped past trees and through bushes—anything to get as far away as possible from the sound of Gorzan's voice. When he finally thought he was safe, he paused to take a breath.

But to his dismay, not far in the distance, he could hear Gorzan echoing after him. "Hey, Wilhurt! *Willlllhurt!* Come back! I think somebody needs a *huuuuuuug!*"

BASIC TRAINING

I t was afternoon at the Lion Camp. Laval, the Lion Prince, paced back and forth, very, very frustrated. "I can't believe the Gorillas," he muttered to himself. "They just do whatever they want!"

Earlier that morning, Laval and a small group of Lion Troops had delivered CHI to the Gorilla Tribe. Just as they had reached the camp, a band of Crocs attacked them! Laval had ordered his troops into battle formations, but the Gorillas . . . well, they had kind of done their own thing. When Laval told them to charge, they swung through the trees. When Laval tossed them CHI Orbs, they missed catching them and dropped bananas on the Crocs' heads instead.

We were lucky to beat the Crocs at all with the way they fought, Laval thought bitterly. *And next time, we might not be so lucky. It could be worse than just a single battle. We could lose control of all of the CHI in Chima!*

Laval was still pacing angrily when his father, King LaGravis, put a hand on his shoulder. "What's the matter, Son?" he asked. "You seem worried."

"It's the Gorillas," Laval answered. "They just . . . they won't listen!"

"Listen to what?" LaGravis frowned.

"Every time we go into a fight with the Crocodiles and the Wolves, the Gorillas just do whatever they like," Laval complained. "I give them orders, but they do the exact opposite. You never know where they will be on the battlefield at any moment, or what they will be doing. They have no discipline!"

LaGravis smiled. Here was his son, the reckless and headstrong Lion Prince, complaining about someone else acting the same way. *Maybe*, he thought, *this would be a good time for Laval to learn a lesson.*

"You know, you're right," LaGravis said. "Someone needs to teach them how to march and drill and fight as a unit."

Laval nodded eagerly. "Exactly! I figured I would ask Longtooth to do it. He has a lot of experience, and—"

"No," LaGravis said, shaking his head. "I need Longtooth here. You should train them, Laval."

"Me?" Laval replied, shocked. "But I . . ."

"The Gorillas trust you," LaGravis said firmly. "You are the only Lion that can train them properly."

"I guess so," Laval said slowly. Then he squared his shoulders. "All right, Dad. I'll do it. I'll train the Gorillas. You can count on me."

"I know I can, Son," LaGravis replied. As he walked away, a small grin crossed the king's face. This was going to be an important lesson for the young Lion Prince.

"You want to teach us something?" Gorzan said. He was hanging upside down on a tree branch, his eyes closed. He had been meditating on the nature of the Great Mellow when Laval showed up.

"That's right," Laval said. "I want you and the other Gorillas to show up tomorrow morning at the big field just south of the creek. We'll start training then."

"Gorillas just love to learn new things," Gorzan answered. "It's all part of the big tapestry that is life in Chima."

"Yeah, sure," Laval replied quickly. "Just remember, tomorrow morning."

The next day, Laval arrived at the field to find a small group of Gorillas waiting for him. But it wasn't all of the fighters from the tribe. And the ones who had shown up weren't exactly ready for training. Some were lying in the grass at the edge of the field. Others were sniffing flowers or pointing up at the clouds.

"Gorzan, where is everyone?" Laval asked, annoyed. "This is important. Everyone needs to be here."

"It wasn't the right time for some of the brothers," Gorzan answered. "They have other roles to play in the Great Mellow, at least until lunch. But we're all ready to learn whatever you want to teach us."

"All right." Laval sighed. He could tell this wasn't going to be easy. "We'll just have to make do. Everybody, on your feet."

One by one, the Gorillas stood up. They didn't seem in any particular hurry. Some stretched, others grabbed fruit from nearby branches. A few even started singing.

"Quiet!" Laval ordered. "Now pay attention. We're going to start with drills. Everyone get into a line."

About three-quarters of the Gorillas got into a straight line. The rest formed a crazy, sort of zigzag pattern.

"What are they doing?" Laval asked.

"They're making a line," Gorzan said.

"That's not a line," Laval said. "That's a zigzag."

"To you, maybe." Gorzan smiled. "But to them, that's what a line looks like."

Laval smacked his head. "That doesn't make sense. Everyone knows what a line looks like!"

"There's room in the Great Mellow for all sorts of lines," Gorzan said. A few of the other Gorillas nodded their heads.

Laval sighed. "Okay, fine. Everyone form a . . . mellow line. Now when I say 'turn left,' everybody turn left. Understand?"

The Gorillas nodded.

"Turn left!" Laval ordered.

Half the Gorillas turned left. The other half turned to the right.

"No, no!" Laval burst out. "Left. I said left!"

"But we did turn left," Gorzan insisted.

Laval groaned. "Don't you guys even know your left from your right?"

Gorzan walked up to Laval and put his hand on his shoulder. "Brother, turn to your left, then back to face me."

Laval did as he was asked. When he was looking at Gorzan again, the Gorilla said, "Now what did you see?"

"The big bush near the creek," Laval answered.

"Good. Now this time, turn your back to me."

When Laval had done so, Gorzan said, "Turn to your left again."

Laval turned. Now he saw the fruit trees that dotted the big, open field.

"You turned left twice, Laval," Gorzan explained, "and both times you faced in a different direction and saw a different part of the world. But which turn was truly to the left?"

Laval clenched his teeth. He knew the Gorillas meant well. But the battlefield was no place for philosophy or open interpretation. The battlefield needed discipline and order!

"Fine," Laval said. "Let's try a different approach."

"What will you teach us now?" Gorzan asked brightly.

Laval turned to face the big Gorilla and went into a battle stance. "Pretend I'm a Crocodile out to steal your CHI. Now stop me!"

"Oh, good. A game." Gorzan grinned.

Laval, for his part, had this all figured out. *The moment he charges, I'll duck out of the way*, he thought. *Then I'll grab Gorzan's arm and use the leverage to send him flying. This will impress the other Gorillas so much that they'll want to listen to me!*

Gorzan charged. Laval sidestepped, grabbed the Gorilla's arm, and pulled. But to his surprise, Gorzan didn't budge. He pulled some more. After a few minutes, he tried pushing. Gorzan didn't move an inch.

"I think I won," Gorzan pointed out.

Laval sat down on a rock and put his chin in his hands. This was getting him nowhere. The Gorillas just didn't understand the importance of learning basic tactics to fight their enemies.

But I promised Dad, Laval thought. *So no matter what, I have to train the Gorillas! Somehow.*

"Okay, next exercise," Laval said, determined.

"Suppose there are Crocs hiding in the creek back there. You need to sneak up and surprise them, and then—"

"Sneak?" asked one of the Gorillas.

"You know, sneak," Laval said. "Get down on your bellies and crawl along the ground so you can't be seen."

Laval had never seen so many shocked expressions at one time before. One of the larger Gorillas raised his hand. "Um, we can't do that," he said. "We would be crushing all the grass and flowers. Besides, Gorillas don't sneak."

"Why not?" Laval asked impatiently.

Gorzan picked up a large, fallen tree branch off the ground and snapped it in half. The two pieces landed at his feet with a loud *thunk*. "We don't need to," he said happily.

Laval looked down at the ground and counted to ten. His father had once told him it was a good way to keep his temper under control. In this case, he ended up having to count to one hundred.

"Fine, let's try a battle simulation with no sneaking," Laval said finally. "I will go hide. You try to find me. It will be good practice for tracking down Croc Spies. Close your eyes and count to . . . whatever number you guys want to count to."

The Gorillas dutifully closed their eyes. Laval ran off toward the creek and hid in the high grass. Five minutes went by, then ten, then twenty, with no sign of the Gorillas. Finally, Laval poked his head above the grass to see what was happening.

To his dismay, the Gorillas were relaxing again. Laval sprang up and stomped over to them.

"You were supposed to come and look for me!" he cried.

"And we were going to," Gorzan replied. "But then we remembered that, in the Great Mellow, everyone ends up in the place they were meant to be. We didn't want to take you away from where you were, if you were happy there."

"But I wasn't—" Laval exploded angrily. Then he caught himself and calmed his voice. "Okay. Here's something easy. Get together—no, it doesn't have to be in a line—and walk across the field. That's all. Just walk. Can you do that?"

Gorzan looked at the field, then back at Laval. "I don't think so."

"Why not?" cried Laval. "It's simple! Anyone can do it. Look, watch me."

"Laval, I really wouldn't do that—" Gorzan began.

"I know, I know." Laval threw his arms up in the air. "I'll trample the flowers, or the Great Mellow wants me to march across some other field miles away from here. Well, I'm going, and you can follow me like warriors or stay here and look at clouds some more."

Before anyone could reply, Laval marched into the field. He was about halfway across when there was a loud *snap*. He looked down to see that his foot was caught in a wooden trap, the kind the Crocodiles sometimes put around the swamp to catch trespassers. It didn't hurt, but it was clamped tight. Laval couldn't get himself free from the snare.

He could have called for help, of course. But after ignoring Gorzan's advice, he would look like a fool if he admitted he had walked right into a trap. Instead, he pretended to be admiring the scenery while he struggled to wrench his foot loose.

After a few minutes, Gorzan asked, "Why have you stopped?"

"Oh, I just . . . thought I'd see what all the fuss was over these flowers," Laval answered, trying to sound like nothing unusual was happening. "I might, um, stay here for a while."

Gorzan looked at the other Gorillas. He didn't have to say a word. They all knew what to do.

In one fluid motion, three Gorillas swung up into the trees. They moved swiftly along the branches, passing from limb to limb. Finally, they reached the place where Laval was trapped. Moving like clockwork, one Gorilla

dropped to the ground while the other two formed a chain from the branch above. The first Gorilla used his massive strength to pry open the trap, while the one hanging from the tree scooped Laval up into the air. The whole rescue mission took less than thirty seconds.

Laval watched, amazed. He had seen the Gorillas in battle and knew they could fight. But he had never seen them in this kind of action. Without an order being given, they acted like a well-trained squad.

Once Laval was back with the Gorillas, he turned to Gorzan. "That was amazing," he said in awe. "If you can do that, why couldn't you do the things I was asking you to do before?"

"We could have," Gorzan admitted. "But we aren't Lions, Laval. We have our own way of doing things. We listen to the wind, the grass, and our own instincts rather than orders. And you should have listened to us. We knew the Crocodiles had been busy in that field. That could only mean trouble."

Laval thought about what Gorzan was saying.

He had been trying to get the Gorillas to train in the same way Lions did. *Maybe I was just getting frustrated with the Gorillas on the battlefield because they don't fight like Lions do*, he thought. *But it looks like their fighting style is just fine as it is.*

"I came to teach you," Laval said, smiling, "but I think I'm the one who ended up learning something."

"Then maybe we can teach you something else," Gorzan said, his face brightening. "Have you ever looked at clouds? Watched them for a whole afternoon? That one up there looks like Cragger. . . ."

Laval spent the rest of the day with the Gorillas, lying in the grass, just looking up at the sky.

THE AUCTION

"**H**oly Razoli, I must be seeing things!" Rizzo the Raven exclaimed, flying closer to the ground. He couldn't believe his luck. There, curled up on the dirt, was the most valuable item he had ever laid eyes on. It was worth hundreds of trinkets and treasures. Maybe even thousands.

I'm just going to borrow this, he thought, stuffing the parchment in his bag. *I'm sure Longtooth won't mind. And if he does, hey, I'll make him a deal.*

Rizzo smiled and quickly flew away. Today was turning out to be a very good day.

Just this morning, he had visited Longtooth the Lion with one of his best deals yet.

"It's a brand-new Speedor wheel. Powerful as can be!" Rizzo had said, presenting Longtooth with a large round stone. It shimmered with blue CHI energy. "Let's make a deal. For you, half off!"

Longtooth wasn't as enthusiastic. "You sneaky thief," he had growled. "That's *my* Speedor wheel. It went missing last month!"

After a heated shouting match, Longtooth had stalked away with the Speedor wheel in hand. He had managed to get it back for just three trinkets and treasures—a very fair deal, if Rizzo said so himself.

That was when the Raven had spotted it.

A curled parchment was lying on the ground near Longtooth's guard post. It looked normal enough. But scrawled across the top in big letters, it read MONTHLY CHI DELIVERY SCHEDULE.

Rizzo realized it was a map of all the CHI delivery routes the Lions were planning to take that month. Anyone who had this scroll could plan ambushes and thefts for weeks! Of course, the Lions could change the schedule, if they noticed the parchment was missing. But if they didn't notice . . . well, a lot of CHI could wind up in the hands of a clever bunch of thieves.

So now, Rizzo was flying back as fast as his wings could carry him to the Ravens' Camp. A devious smile spread across his face. *I could use the map for myself*, he thought. *But I'd need other Ravens to help me ambush the Lions. And then I'd have to split the profits! No,*

I've got a better idea. It's time for a good old-fashioned auction.

Rizzo was not popular, even for a member of his tribe. Where most Ravens had some depths to which they would not sink, Rizzo had none. Other animals said that he was dishonest, a cheat, a thief, someone who would sell his own grandmother if the price was right. He had to admit they were right about the first three. As for Grandma, he always made sure she got a cut whenever he sold her . . . a small cut, but still, it was something. And one thing no one could deny was that he knew how to make a deal.

Rizzo quietly put out the word that the parchment was up for sale, starting with the Crocodiles. Then he let the Wolves know, too. An auction was no good with only one bidder. As he landed in the field chosen for the auction site, he saw Crooler the Crocodile and Windra the Wolf stalking up to the clearing.

"What's *she* doing here?" Windra snarled, looking Crooler up and down.

"I would ask the same thing," Crooler said, her eyes narrowing at Rizzo. "I thought this was a private sale."

"It is," Rizzo insisted. "A private *auction*. Just you two—no one else. Only my best clients."

Rizzo smiled. "Now, who would like to make me the first offer?"

"Where's the parchment?" Windra asked. "Show it to us first."

Rizzo gulped. "Well, I don't have it with me," he said. "How dumb do you think I am?"

Crooler started to answer, but then changed her mind. "Fine. Let's get this over with," she said. "I bid five trinkets and treasures."

"Ten," said Windra.

"Twenty," snapped Crooler.

"I meant ten a month for the rest of your life," Windra hissed.

"I meant twenty a week for the rest of your life," Crooler countered.

Windra leaned in close to Rizzo. "Sell it to me, or there won't *be* a rest of your life."

Rizzo shuddered.

"Stop bidding, *Wolf*," Crooler threatened.

Windra bared her teeth. "Make me."

"This is getting us nowhere," Crooler said angrily. "I don't like your *auction*, Rizzo. There are other ways to settle this." She stalked away.

Windra watched her go, and then slowly turned toward the Raven. "You know, the pack can be a good friend," she smiled at Rizzo. "Suppose you needed a little . . . protection. Worriz and the Wolves would be happy to take care of that for you. All you have to do is give me that parchment."

Rizzo fluttered into the air. He didn't like having a Wolf's jaws quite so close. "Ravens don't give things away," he whined. "It's against the law."

Windra's smile widened. On her face, it was a frightening expression. "And Wolves don't take 'no' for an answer."

Rizzo flew higher, out of reach. "Uh . . . I've gotta go. Things to do. Deals to make. See you later," he said quickly.

Windra watched him fly away. Then she left, too. Neither of them noticed the figure keeping an eye on them silently from the woods. He was covered in mud to mask his scent. Once Crooler and Windra were out of sight, the figure trotted off after Rizzo.

Rizzo landed on a high rock near the mountains. He had never been in the middle of a deal this big, or this dangerous, before. Two of the nastiest females in Chima both wanted this parchment, and they would go *through* him to get it if necessary. Normally, Rizzo stored all his goods-for-sale in a hollow tree near the Ravens' Camp. But this parchment was too hot to keep in any old tree. He carefully tucked the paper into a crack near the bottom of the rock.

Then he decided to check on his other treasures. *Maybe I'll make a few simple deals to clear my head*, he thought. *Nothing like a good bargain to calm my nerves.*

Rizzo flew down into the woods toward the hollow tree where he kept his best stuff. He knew the way by heart and didn't even bother watching where he flew. So he was quite surprised when he smacked headfirst into a tree.

"Holy Razoli!" cried Rizzo, rubbing his head. "Where did that tree come from?"

After the world stopped spinning, Rizzo noticed something. It wasn't just any tree he had collided with. It was *his* hollow tree. But this wasn't where it always was in the forest. Somebody had moved his tree! Frantic, he peered through a knothole. All his stuff was gone!

"Don't you hate it when trees move?"

Rizzo felt a chill run through him. He turned to see Crooler leaning casually against a rock.

"Good thing your junk wasn't stolen," she said. "It's just scattered around the woods. Sometimes my boys get a little . . . messy."

"Aw, come on," Rizzo groaned. "The other Ravens will have found all my good stuff by now."

"Well, accidents do happen," Crooler said, walking closer. "It would be a shame if any more *accidents* happened, right?"

"Yeah . . ." Rizzo gulped.

"But a parchment can buy protection. So more accidents don't happen. Get it?" she said.

"G-G-Got it," Rizzo stammered.

"Good," said Crooler. "You know what to do."

Rizzo flew home. Now he was *really* worried. If he gave the parchment to Windra, Crooler would drop a tree on him. But if he gave it to Crooler, he would have the Wolf Pack chasing him forever. And if he *gave* it to anyone, instead of selling it, Razar and the Ravens would laugh him out of the nest!

By that evening, Rizzo still hadn't figured out what to do. He decided to sleep on it. Maybe he would come up with the best deal ever for the parchment after a full night's sleep.

All night, Rizzo had bad dreams. He kept thinking Windra and Crooler had come to the Raven Camp. They were searching for the parchment. When they couldn't

find it, he dreamed that they decided to take *him* instead. Then they got into an argument over who got to "persuade" him to talk first.

When Rizzo woke up the next morning, the camp was in chaos. There were Wolf footprints all over the ground below the nests. Someone had dripped swamp water on Razar's ledgers. And the Ravens were flying about in a panic. Shocked, Rizzo realized it hadn't been a dream: The Wolves and the Crocodiles had actually shown up. They had ransacked the Raven Camp looking for the parchment!

That's it, Rizzo thought. *This parchment is too hot for even a Raven to hold on to. I've got to get rid of it!*

Suddenly, Rizzo realized the answer to all his problems. He just had to do what Ravens did best: swindle! It was so simple, he wondered why he hadn't thought of it before.

"I'll sell them both fake copies of the CHI delivery schedule!" he exclaimed.

Rizzo set to work forging new schedules on pieces of parchment. He made two: one for the Crocodiles, and one for the Wolves. They were completely different from each other, so the two sides wouldn't wind up both at the same site waiting to ambush the Lions. Of course,

neither of the forgeries used information from the real schedule. That way, it wasn't like he was giving anything of real value to either side. The Crocodiles would be happy. The Wolves would be happy. And the Ravens wouldn't kick Rizzo out of the nest for breaking the cardinal rule to never *give* anything away. That made Rizzo happy.

When he was done, Rizzo took one copy to the Wolf Pack. He made a quick deal with Windra: the parchment in exchange for the Wolves' "continued protection."

Then he took the other copy to the swamp and gave it to Crooler in exchange for more "protection."

On his way back to camp, Rizzo felt like a winner. After all, what could go wrong? Even if all the ambushes were failures, both tribes would just assume the Lions had discovered a copy of the schedule had been stolen and so changed their plans. None of it could be traced back to Rizzo.

Phew, Rizzo thought. *That's the last auction I'm holding for a while.*

Three days later, Wilhurt the Wolf was very angry. He had just spent four hours hiding in the woods with the rest of the pack, waiting to ambush the Lions' CHI delivery. But the Lions never showed up. Frustrated, Wilhurt ordered the pack back to camp when they bumped into Crawley and the Crocodiles.

"Lost?" he asked Crawley with a sneer.

"No," Crawley snapped. "We were waiting to ambush Laval and take some CHI, but he must have made a new

plan. Either that, or the schedule we got from Rizzo is wrong."

"The schedule *you* got . . . ?" Wilhurt exclaimed. "What are you talking about? *We* got the CHI schedule from Rizzo. It said to wait by the twin oak trees today, but we never saw any Lions."

"Ours said to wait by the bend in the creek," Crawley said. His eyes narrowed. "Are you thinking what I'm thinking?"

"I smell a Raven," Wilhurt snarled.

The next day, Rizzo was just about to head to the Beavers' dam to sell them some wood when he heard rustling in the bushes behind him. Rizzo tried to take off, but before he could get away, a hand grabbed his leg. Then a second hand grabbed his other leg.

It was Windra and Crooler. And they didn't look happy.

"Uh, hello," Rizzo said. "What can I do for you charming ladies today?"

Windra growled. "Those CHI schedules you sold us—"

"Were fakes!" Crooler finished.

"What?" exclaimed Rizzo, putting on his most innocent expression. "I'm shocked. Shocked! I promise you, I won't rest until I find out what happened."

"I promise you won't rest, either," Windra said through gritted teeth.

"Take us to the real parchment now, Raven," said Crooler, "or else."

"Or else?" gulped Rizzo.

"You're a fast talker," Crooler said. "Try talking when your beak's upside down."

No matter how much Rizzo hated giving things away, he *really* didn't want to find out what Windra and Crooler were capable of. He led them to the rock where he had hidden the parchment. Windra flipped it over and grabbed the paper. Crooler snatched it out of her hand.

"Give me that!" snapped Windra.

"Make me," taunted Crooler.

"Fine," Windra said. "Then let's look at it together. We're your *allies*, remember? We'll help you attack the Lions. That is, if we're still on the same side."

Begrudgingly, Crooler allowed Windra to look over her shoulder as she read the parchment. *"Monthly Schedule,"* she read aloud. *"Task One: Clean out caves. Task Two: Train with Leonidas. Task Three: Trick Wolves, Crocodiles, and Rizzo with a fake parchment . . ."*

Crooler crumpled the paper up in her claws. "This isn't a CHI delivery schedule—it's a to-do list!" she cried.

"But I don't understand," Rizzo sputtered, snatching away the parchment. "It was real. I saw it with my own two eyes. And I left it right here!"

As the three animals argued, none of them noticed the small group of Lions hidden off to the side, laughing quietly.

"See?" Longtooth said to his soldiers. "I told you I would handle it."

"But how did you know where the parchment was hidden?" one of the Lions asked.

"It was easy," Longtooth explained. "I knew that sneaky Raven was behind it. But as slippery as Ravens are, they're no match for a Lion's hunting skills. I just waited until Rizzo went to sell it, which I knew he would, and followed him to where he had hidden it. I switched out the real parchment yesterday. It was a piece of cake."

"Looks like you taught that Raven a lesson." The Lions grinned as they heard Rizzo trying to sweet-talk Crooler and Windra into believing it was all a big misunderstanding.

"Now, ladies," Rizzo was saying, "don't worry. I'm sure we can work something out."

"You're right, we will," Crooler said as she and Windra walked closer.

With a squawk, Rizzo raced away as fast as his legs would carry him. Windra and Crooler chased close behind.

"You won't get away with this, Raven!" they both shouted after him.

One of the Lions looked at Longtooth. "Think he'll be all right?" he asked.

Longtooth nodded. "Eh, he'll be fine," he said. "After all, if there's one thing we know Rizzo is an expert at, it's making a deal."